Brave Sir Laughalot

Written by Morgan Matthews
Illustrated by Mary Alice Baer

Troll Associates

Library of Congress Cataloging in Publication Data

Matthews, Morgan.
    Brave Sir Laughalot.

    Summary: Sir Laughalot rides out in search of
adventure, but never realizes how much good he does.
    [1. Knights and knighthood—Fiction. 2. Stories in
rhyme] I. Baer, Mary Alice, ill. II. Title.
PZ8.3.M44Br   1986   [E]   85-14010
ISBN 0-8167-0594-1 (lib. bdg.)
ISBN 0-8167-0595-X (pbk.)

Brave
Sir Laughalot

This is a tale of long ago,
about a knight who wanted
    to be brave.
He went out to look for adventure.
But he found no one to save.

Who was that brave knight?
His name was Sir Laughalot.
Where did he live?
He lived in old Camelot.

Sir Laughalot?
What a silly name for a knight!
But Sir Laughalot made
    everyone laugh.
So his silly name was just right.

In Camelot were many knights.
And they had many names.
They fought dragons, giants, and
    witches.
And they told of their fame.

The knights told of their adventures.
They bragged day after day.
But Sir Laughalot did not brag.
For he had nothing to say.

The others had fought many battles.
Sir Laughalot had not.
So the other knights all laughed
       at him.
They laughed and laughed a lot.

It is not nice to laugh at others.
Bragging is not good.
Sir Laughalot wanted to be brave.
And he would if he could.

"I will find adventure," he said.
"I will go right away!
I do not want to brag and brag.
But I *do* want something to say."

Sir Laughalot said, "Before I go,
    I'll shine my sword, of course."
Then he put on his armor.
And he got on his horse!

"Look out witches!
Look out giants and dragons,"
    he cried.
"Brave Sir Laughalot is on his way.
You had better hide."

Away rode the silly knight.
Clank went the sword at his side.
Clink-clunk went his armor.
What a noisy ride!

On and on rode Sir Laughalot.
He wanted to do a brave deed.
So he called, "Come out, witches
      and dragons.
You are what I need!"

16

What did Sir Laughalot find?
What he found was not good.
Where he rode was very scary.
It was a scary old wood.

Who lived there?
Who lived in the dark and
    dismal wood?
A scary old witch lived there.
And witches are not good.

"What is that silly noise?" cried
    the witch.
"Who is calling my name?
Is a brave knight calling me?
Does he look for fame?"

Out of the woods came the witch.
She looked straight at the knight.
Sir Laughalot saw the scary witch.
Oh what a terrible fright!

Sir Laughalot reached for his sword.
He waved it at the witch.
Then *oops*, he fell off of his horse—
straight into a ditch!

"What a noisy knight," said the witch.
"And a silly one, too."
She laughed at him, and then she said,
"A spell will fix you!"

Sir Laughalot was frightened.
Now he wanted to hide.
He was much too scared to fight.
So he just turned aside.

The spell nicked his armor.
But the armor was shiny and good.
The armor turned away the spell.
The spell went into the wood.
And then something happened.
The spell went from bad to good!

The woods were now good.
The witch was good, too.
"What a brave knight," said the
good witch.
"What a good deed to do.
I will go and tell of your fame.
I will brag about you."

"Brag about me?" said Sir Laughalot.
He did not know what to say.
He did not know what he had done.
So he just rode away.

He rode and rode in the hot sun.
On he went to a lake.
"It is too, too hot," he said.
"A dip is what I will take."

Off went his armor.
He left it in the sun.
"I am going in the lake," said he.
"I'll be back when I am done."

By the lake lived a giant.
He saw the armor there.
"I will fix that knight," said the giant.
"I will give him a scare."

Up to the armor went the giant.
Said he, "This armor I will take."
The giant laughed and laughed
    some more.
"I will throw it in the lake."

The sun was very hot.
The armor was hot, too.
The giant took the armor.
What a silly thing to do!

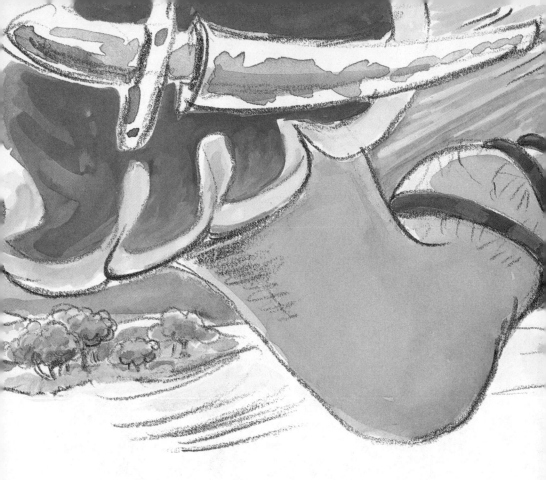

"Ouch!" cried the giant.
"Hot armor is not good.
Ouch! Ouch! Ouch!" he cried.
And off he ran into the wood.
A man saw the giant run away.
He saw Sir Laughalot, too.
"Frightening a giant," said the man.
"What a brave deed to do!"

Fighting witches and giants?
Doing deeds very brave?
It could not be Sir Laughalot.
He could find no one to save.

"Now I am not hot," said the knight.
"I'm ready to do a brave deed."
He put back on his armor
and climbed back on his steed.

"Look out witches!
Look out giants and dragons,"
    he cried.
"Brave Sir Laughalot is coming.
You had better hide."

Sir Laughalot rode and rode.
He rode into a town.
But he did not see anyone.
There was no one around.

"Why is everyone hiding?" called
    the knight.
"Why is no one here?"
"I will tell you why," called a man.
"There is a dragon near."

"A dragon," said Sir Laughalot.
"A brave deed I will do.
I will find that scary dragon.
And I will fight it just for you."

He looked for the dragon.
He looked here and there.
"Where is that dragon?" said Sir Laughalot.
"I have looked everywhere."

"I will go up a hill," he said.
"From a hill it is easy to see.
Then I will see the dragon.
But the dragon will not see me."

Up, up, up the hill he went.
But then Sir Laughalot stumbled.
Rocks started to fall down.
Down the hill they tumbled.

The dragon lived by the hill.
There was a cave in its side.
The dragon lived in the cave.
It went there to hide.

Lots and lots of rocks fell.
Rocks filled up the cave.
The awful dragon could not get out.
And so the town was saved!

Silly Sir Laughalot stumbled
      and tumbled.
Down, down he went. Clink! Clunk!
He fell down the hill.
Clink! Clank! Thunk!

Oh, what a silly knight!
Oh, what a frightful day!
Oh, what a bad fall!
What could Sir Laughalot say?

"I fought no dragon," said the
    sad knight.
"My adventures are all done.
Now I must return to Camelot.
And that will *not* be fun."

Sir Laughalot rode to Camelot,
where they knew of his fame.
He had fought a witch, a giant,
    and a dragon.
So no one laughed when he came.

That day no other knights bragged.
What could they say?
Sir Laughalot kept his brave
    tales to himself.
And so did they.